Hair Love

For the daughters who never grow too old to
need a father's helping hand
and the fathers who love to be needed
—M. C.

For my dad and his excellent braiding skills
—V. H.

Kokila
An imprint of Penguin Random House LLC, New York

Text copyright © 2019 by Matthew A. Cherry.
Illustrations copyright © 2019 by Vashti Harrison.

Visit us online at
penguinrandomhouse.com

CIP data is available.

Manufactured in China
ISBN 9780525553366

16

Design by Jasmin Rubero
Text set in Carre Noir Pro

The art for this book was created digitally.

Hair Love

Matthew A. Cherry ✳ illustrations by **Vashti Harrison**

Kokila

My name is Zuri, and I have hair that has a mind of its own.
It kinks, coils, and curls every which way.

Daddy tells me it is beautiful.
That makes me proud.
I love that my hair lets me be me!

In funky braids with beads,
I am a princess.

And when my hair is in two puffs,
I am above the clouds like a superhero.

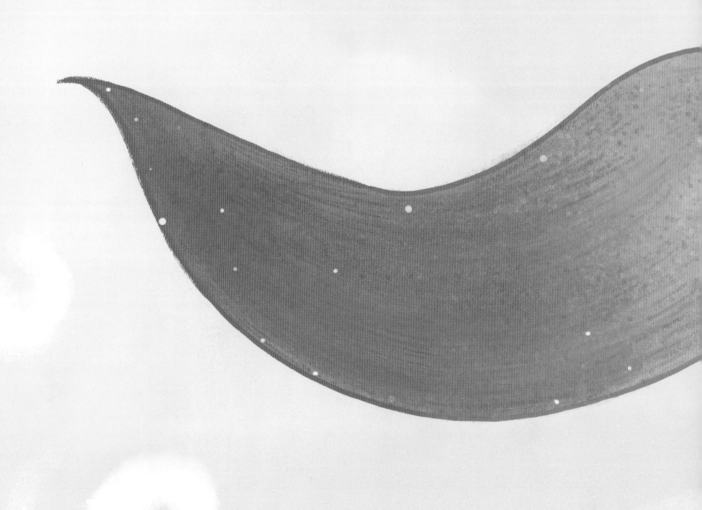

My hair even does magic tricks.
One day Rocky and I were playing
outside when along came the rain.

From large to small it went.
Presto! Just like that!

There is nothing my hair can't do!

Today I woke up extra early all by myself.

I was too excited to sleep.

It's a big day!

Daddy was still sleeping.

"Shh," I said to Rocky as we tiptoed past him.

Lately Daddy has been worn-out!

He makes me breakfast,
takes me to school,
goes to work, picks me up,
and yesterday we went for
a bike ride around the park.

I think he needs a break.

Because today is special,
I want a *perfect* hairstyle.
This calls for a
professional's touch.

"Paws off, Rocky!"

Daddy heard the crash.
"Zuri, what on earth?"
he asked.

"I was only trying to help," I said.

Daddy smiled. "Can I help, too? It'll be a piece of cake, Zuzu."

The first style was a big NO WAY.

The second was no better.

"No, Daddy."

Then Daddy tried slicking my hair
back into two puffs.

"Ouch!"
Daddy yelled.

"Wait a minute," Daddy said as he reached into the drawer and pulled out a pick.

"Ta-da!"

"Daddy, really?" I said.

"I'll be right back," he promised.

"Now. How's that?" he asked,
pulling a hat down over my eyes.

"Daddy, come on. We can do
better than that."

"I really need my hair to be special."

"Don't worry," he said,
"we'll figure this out."

Then I had a great idea.

Daddy gathered all the tools
we needed, and we were set!

Watching carefully . . .

Daddy combed,

parted, oiled, and twisted.

He nailed it!

Funky puff buns!
Pretty, pretty, and so much fun.
Rocky approved, too!

CLICK

I put on my superhero cape as the final touch to a perfect look.

"Where's my Zuzu?" Mommy called from the door.
She could not get in the house fast enough.

"Mommy!"

"You've got to be the prettiest supergirl I have ever seen," she said.

"And your hair is beautiful, Zuri.
Who did it?"
I looked at Daddy and beamed.

Mommy smiled. "Very nice."
"Thank you. We learned from the best,"
Daddy said as he gave her a big hug.

My hair is Mommy, Daddy, and me.
It's hair love!